J
chapter
ASK
red
dots
INTO

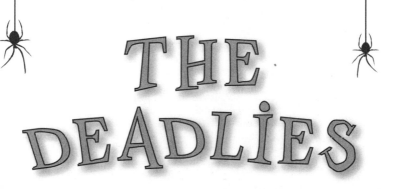

THE
DEADLIES

FELIX TAKES THE STAGE

by **KATHRYN LASKY**

illustrated by **STEPHEN GILPIN**

Scholastic Press / New York

To Greta Binford, who has
taught me to love spiders
—KL

The author gratefully acknowledges Dr. Greta Binford, Professor of Biology at Lewis & Clark College, for her help with the spider research in this book.

Library of Congress Cataloguing-in-Publication Data
Lasky, Kathryn.
Felix takes the stage / by Kathryn Lasky.
p. cm. — (The Deadlies)
Summary: Having been discovered, a family of poisonous but friendly
brown recluse spiders must flee their cozy home in a symphony hall and
go searching for a new place to live.
ISBN-13: 978-0-545-11681-7
ISBN-10: 0-545-11681-3
[1. Brown recluse spider — Fiction.   2. Spiders — Fiction.   3. Home —
Fiction.]   I. Title.
PZ7.L3274Fe 2010
[Fic] — dc22
2009033149
10 9 8 7 6 5 4 3 2 1   10 11 12 13 14
Printed in the U.S.A.   23
First edition, May 2010
The text is set in Apollo MT.
The display type is set in Woodrow.
Book design by Lillie Howard

PROLOGUE

For Felix, the best part of the night came when the concert had ended. The lights in the grand symphony hall had dimmed. The audience had gone home, as had the members of the orchestra with their instruments. But the Maestro stayed on. Still at his podium, he raised his baton to conduct a phantom orchestra. And so in a strange way the music lingered, at least for Felix. He knew exactly which part the Maestro would go over with the mute orchestra — the second movement of Brahms's Symphony no. 3. The musicians had not done their best with it. And Felix knew that the Maestro probably blamed himself. He would rehearse it now, silently, as was his custom after a less than perfect performance.

Felix was all eyes — all six of them riveted on the symphony conductor he worshipped. He loved music. He felt it with every nano-hair on his eight legs. And now he dared to creep out from behind the music stand, where he had hidden between the pages of the score.

If I could only ride the baton, I could feel the passion of the notes, Felix thought.

Go for it! A tiny voice in his head urged.

But riding the baton would break his mother's most basic rule — never, *ever* reveal yourself to human beings. Her words had been repeated over and over until they threaded through his mind. "We are recluses; that is the name of our species. We hide!"

Felix felt a slight wobble in at least four of his eight legs. Half of him wanted to be a good spiderling and obey his mother, but the other half . . . oh, that other half yearned to be an artist!

Felix understood his mother's reasoning. The venom of brown recluse spiders was one of the most toxic on earth. It was natural that humans feared them, even though no one in his family had EVER attacked anyone. But Felix was deeply musical. He lived in a philharmonic hall and yet his mother had forbidden him to get anywhere near the great conductor. It seemed to

Felix that his mom was as scared of humans as humans were of them.

It made no sense. Leon Brinsky was his hero. The man was a genius. *I don't have to talk to him,* Felix thought. *I'm not asking for his autograph. I just want to feel the motion of the baton. That's all, for crying out loud!*

And with that, Felix backed around. The muscles of his spinnerets began to force liquid silk up toward his spigots. Another few seconds and he'd have a hoist line to swing up to the baton. *Now I'll know Brahms!*

It was Felix's last thought before the accident.

"Mom!!!" he screeched in pain.

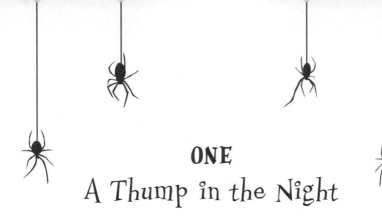

ONE
A Thump in the Night

Felix's mother, Edith, was tending her rather disorderly web in the basement when she felt the thump. A rain of dust and debris fell down on the small section of the web that she had planned to use for "circle time" with her young brood. This was a concept Edith had learned about at the Martin Luther King Jr. Elementary School in Phoenix, Arizona. The young kindergartners and their teacher would all sit on the floor and share ideas and stories. Edith was trying very hard to make a circular area, but brown recluse spiders were not known for their neat webs.

Edith had been very fond of that kindergarten teacher, Ms. Lafferty. She loved the stories

Ms. Lafferty told that drew out even the shyest kindergartner. When the children were not paying attention, Ms. Lafferty would say, "All eyes on me!" Edith wanted to have circle time like that with her own children — Jo Bell, Felix, and little Julep. All eighteen of their eyes on her.

Ms. Lafferty had deeply influenced Edith. In her own mind, Edith thought of her children as being the ages and grades of schoolchildren. Julep, the youngest, was a kindergartner, perhaps on occasion pre-K. Felix was an elementary

school kid. Jo Bell, the oldest, was junior high age but yearning to be considered a high school girl.

Just then, Edith heard the awful thump. *No!* she thought. She instinctively drew her fangs in tighter.

"Felix!" she called out. "Felix, you didn't!"

Felix picked up the anguish in his mother's voice as he scuttled and skibbled his way down an air-conditioning vent to the basement.

She can't think I actually killed him — not on purpose!

"Mom!" he called as he arrived at the web. "All I did was —"

"It doesn't matter. He's dead, right?"

"He only saw me. That's all!"

"Look at him," Jo Bell wailed. "Felix is bleeding!"

"Bleeding? Where?" Edith asked.

"Mommy, Felix's lost a leg!" Julep cried.

"Oh, mercy!" Edith swung down from the messy circle she had been making. There were pale blue drops on the floor where Felix had now collapsed. "Don't worry, darling. I'll staunch this blood in a second."

She quickly tore a swathe from the web she had been spinning and began to bandage the wound. The bleeding stopped.

"Mom, I did NOT bite him. I really didn't. He just collapsed as a reaction to seeing me. I kept my fangs tucked, I swear! Even when he sliced down with his baton — I never thought of a baton as a weapon — it was art . . . art."

"Don't talk, nubkins. You're too weak."

"But I thought it was art. Mom, I'm not a killer."

"No, darling. I know that."

She has to understand that whatever happened was by accident! Just an accident.

"Felix, you lost a leg for art. You almost died for art!" Julep wailed.

"There will be no talking of death. Stop that right now! Felix will survive." Edith spoke fiercely. "Felix's only crime was that he showed himself."

"But, Mom, it can't be a *crime* to be seen," Felix objected.

"I misspoke, dear. I didn't mean *crime*. I meant inappropriate behavior."

But Felix suspected his mother *did* think it was a crime to be seen. Good behavior in his mother's mind was hiding in the dimmest, darkest places imaginable. Then an odd thought struck Felix. *I'm not a criminal, but perhaps I am not a recluse either.* An argument began within Felix. For if he was not a recluse, which by definition meant one who avoided contact with others, did that mean he was not a member of his species — the brown recluse spider? Was he denying his species or just his personality?

"I'll never be able to conduct with only seven legs anyway," Felix muttered.

"How will he hunt? How will he move with only seven?" Jo Bell asked.

"Enough of that, young lady!" Edith took a deep breath. "Felix will live. He will hunt. He will even conduct. If you knew the first thing about spider biology, you would know that a young spider is perfectly capable of regrowing a limb during his next molt."

"Really, Mom?" Felix asked.

"Really." Edith paused. "Now, we're going to have to get out of here, children. There's no choice." She paused again, then looked into the eighteen eyes of her children. "You know what I mean!"

"It's the E word, isn't it?" Jo Bell said.

"Yes, exterminators."

"Oh, no!" whispered Julep. They had all heard about the terrible humans who came in white suits with gleaming white helmets and hoses, but the children had never seen them. However, Edith had. She didn't talk about it much. When the children asked her questions, she was always quite vague. The E-Men were a subject the whole family avoided.

"Before we leave, I want to check on the Maestro. If he's not dead, maybe we can help him. Jo Bell!"

"Yes, Mom."

"Get Fat Cat now. Hop to it!"

TWO
Fat Cat

With the exception of the elementary school where Edith once lived, she'd always had a penchant for theatrical places — grand old movie palaces, theaters, opera houses — the more ornate the better. Therefore, she was familiar with the tradition of theater cats. These cats slinked about backstage, a soothing presence for nervous performers and an effective way to keep down the mouse population. Perhaps the most notorious of these felines was Fat Cat's distant cousin Boy Cat, who had hopped down from the stage into the empty front row seat during *The Phantom of the Opera,* perched next to Princess Margaret, and then proceeded to eat her bouquet.

Fat Cat, or Fatty, as he was fondly called, was a lazy caramel-colored Manx and had long been the "house cat" at the philharmonic hall. He had arrived some years before on a cruise ship that specialized in theater on the high seas. The seas, however, got a bit too high and the drama — well, too dramatic — when the ship sprang a leak. Fatty had washed up in a bucket on the shore of Venice Beach in California.

He had arrived at the symphony hall shortly before Edith. The poor spider was clearly exhausted when she staggered into Fatty's basement.

But Fatty was drawn to her immediately. Even sleepy, she had a charm..

"Don't worry! Don't worry!" she kept telling him. "It's nothing. Nothing! I'll be fine in a few hours. But I'm too tired to make a web at the moment. "

"Rest here, madame." Fatty wiggled an ear.

"Oh, how kind."

"Here, I'll help you." Fatty pressed his furry cheek against the floor so Edith could climb into his left ear.

A few hours later, Edith had spun a silken sac into which she had deposited her eggs. "You don't mind? Do you?"

"No, not at all," Fatty replied, although it was rather like having cotton plugs in his ear.

And then a few weeks later, what Edith referred to as "nothing" became "something." Something that Fatty would always think of as a miracle. For that evening, during a stirring cello performance, Edith's eggs hatched. Jo Bell first, then Felix, and finally Julep almost an hour later. It was a small brood, most likely because of how tired Edith had been. She later explained that her husband had died shortly after she found out that the children were coming. Without Fatty, she might not have managed on her own.

Fatty became the children's godspider. One did not have to be a spider to assume this role of mentor, second-opinion giver, and protector. Kindness and wisdom were Edith's main requirements. Edith herself had had a pig for her godspider, a pig named Charlotte, who oddly enough had been named for a famous spider in literature. If Fat Cat had any flaws, it was a tendency toward laziness that left him a little chubby.

"Fatty! At last. We've had a disaster!" Edith began.

Fatty caught sight of Felix and blinked. "What in the name of . . ."

Edith sighed. "Did you hear that thump?"

"Yes." Fatty said, then purred with deep apprehension. "Not the . . ."

Edith nodded wordlessly.

"We must check on the Maestro at once!" Fat Cat exclaimed.

"That's why I sent for you. If he is not d-e-a-d"— She could not say the dreadful word. She had to spell it out, although all of her children could spell — "if he isn't, we must do something to save him."

"Of course." Fat Cat nodded.

Edith turned to Felix. "Felix, we're going upstairs to the stage and investigate. You stay here."

"I don't think I have much choice, Mom. Remember, I've lost a leg."

"Yes, dear, but that eighth leg will grow back. Next molt. Now I'm going to wrap that bandage a bit tighter." Edith made a grimace and began squeezing out some more liquid silk. Then, like the most superb seamstress, she began to weave an outer layer around Felix's wound.

"Marvelous, simply marvelous!" Fatty purred in wonder as he watched Edith with her son.

"All right, we're off!" Edith said as she tied the last knot. "The girls and I will take the air vents, Fatty. You take the stairs. We'll meet at the podium."

And so the cat and the three spiders made their separate ways toward the stage, where the Maestro lay in a heap.

Let him not be dead! Let him not be dead!
Edith prayed to a nameless spider god of silk
and venom. Edith was not one to complain or
whine, but in bad moments, she did feel that
there was something very sad about being so
misunderstood. Not simply misunderstood but
reviled. It seemed preposterous to Edith that
humans feared her as much as they feared
great white sharks. *We're not mean,* Edith
thought mournfully. *We just happen to be
extremely venomous.*

THREE
A Calling Card

Brown *recluse spiders,* Edith thought, *rarely waste our venom on things we cannot eat.* What lay before her was definitely indigestible. The Maestro was a mountain of a man. The immense expanse of his starched white dress shirt lofted into the dim light like an alpine field. The pages of his score for the Brahms symphony were scattered about like patches of snow at a mountain base. And now the time had come to climb. "All right, children, I want you to start paying out your number one quality silk. We're going to need the best haul lines ever."

"Mom, we've never spun that kind of silk," Julep said.

She didn't want to alarm her children, but this was an alarming situation and it seemed Julep was on the brink of one of her pre-K moments.

"Julep, don't whine. Just do it! This is a matter of life and death." Edith paused. "Now prepare to ascend!" The message was clear. *This is serious business!*

Fatty watched as the three spiders entered a kind of deep trance. Soon the silk was paid out and he saw the little spider family, led by the intrepid Edith, begin their ascent. Unlike human mountain climbers, their ropes never ever twisted and were hundreds of times stronger per weight and strand, although many times thinner. But to Fatty, this was more than mountain climbing. The air was suddenly filled with flowing rivulets of silk, and the three spiders, as graceful as aerial artists, swung through the air on glimmering threads. The air seemed to sparkle with their silken choreography. *Now, this is theater!* Fatty thought.

"Summit!" Edith called down. The leg hairs of spiders contain some of the most highly refined sensors of any animal on earth. They can detect the slightest vibration of a microscopic insect in a web. Edith quickly scuttled across the Maestro's belly and crawled up a gully formed by a pleat of his dress shirt. She wanted to stand over his heart to see if she could confirm a pulse.

Hardly a quarter way up the pleat gully, Edith felt distant heartbeats, though they were somewhat irregular. Relief swept through her entire body, from fangs to spinnerets.

"Heartbeat confirmed!" she cried. "The Maestro lives! Quick, children, down we go. I must consult with Fatty at base camp."

And so Edith swung herself onto the two parallel threads of silk and began a controlled but speedy downward slide. She was followed by Jo Bell and Julep, who argued about who got to go first. "You always go before me," Julep complained.

"Don't whine! I'm older."

"That's no excuse."

Fatty shouted up, "Stop your bickering, both of you!"

"So, Fatty, he lives. Did you find any signs of bites, any fang marks at all?" Edith asked.

"Unconsciously, Felix's fangs could have shot out — just a reaction."

"No, Edith," Fatty said slowly, but there was a certain tension in his voice. "There was no sign of injury — not of injury inflicted by Felix."

"It was obviously fear that made the Maestro faint," Edith said confidently.

"Yes, he definitely fainted."

"But what, Fatty?"

Fatty looked down at the starched white cuff that extended from the sleeve of the Maestro's tuxedo jacket. All six of Edith's eyes focused on the two pale blue drops at the very edge of the cuff. Felix's blood! Despite her eight legs, she suddenly felt unsteady.

"Mom!" Julep gasped.

"Mother!" Jo Bell said.

"I'll be fine, girls. Just let me catch my breath." She turned to Fat Cat. "Fatty, you know what this means."

"It's like a calling card, isn't it?" the cat answered.

"Yes, exactly — a calling card: 'Brown recluses have been here.'"

"Mom?" Julep said, her voice fraught with alarm. "Will the humans come for us?"

"Yes, I'm afraid so," Edith replied in a dim little voice.

"No hope mopping up the blood, I suppose?" Fatty asked.

"None. It's soaked into the material."

"But, Mom, what are you talking about? The Maestro's not dead," Jo Bell said.

"No, but it will still be the . . ."

"The E word," Julep whispered.

"Yes, children. We haven't much time." Edith swung around to face Fat Cat. "The Maestro might have suffered a heart attack when he saw Felix. Fatty, we have to alert someone. And then the children and I have to skedaddle."

"Oh, Edith!"

"Fatty, no drama! If he has suffered a heart attack, we might be able to save him."

"But how?"

"You're going to have to pull the fire alarm. It's the only way." She paused a moment. "And to put it plainly, children, as soon as they see that blue blood, we'll be on the Most Wanted list. Murder suspects."

"But he's not dead," Jo Bell said.

"It doesn't matter. The E-Men will come within the hour. This place will be sealed off. Fatty, you'll have to leave, too, at least temporarily. That stuff is terrible. It kills spiders, but it won't do you any good either, believe me. I've seen what it can do." Her somber tone was like a death knell.

Fatty heaved a deep sigh. "Yes, yes, I suppose you're right, Edith."

"There's an alarm to stage left, in the wings, by the switch box. Get to it, Fatty."

Julep and Jo Bell gasped as Fatty streaked

across the stage. Never had they seen the old cat move so fast.

Within seconds, the performance hall was reverberating with the screech of the alarm. And in less than two minutes, there was the answering scream of sirens as fire trucks and ambulances tore through the streets of Los Angeles toward the little spider family.

FOUR
On the Road

"**A**re we halfway there yet?" Julep asked.

"Halfway to where?" Jo Bell muttered. "Like Mom really knows where she's going! Gimme a break!"

"Children!" Fat Cat said sharply. "I don't like your tone, and I'm sure your mother doesn't either."

"And don't say 'gimme a break'!" Felix exclaimed. "It's not very sensitive, considering what I have just been through." Felix was being transported aboard Fatty. He was tucked into Fat Cat's ear, which made a furry little reclining lounge chair for him.

"I don't think it's fair that Felix gets to

ride," Julep complained. "I mean, he's still got seven legs."

"Fair!" Felix and Jo Bell exclaimed together.

"Julep," Jo Bell scolded. "Take it back this instant!"

"Sorry," Julep muttered.

"Really sorry?" Jo Bell insisted.

"Okay, I am really sorry, really, really, really sorry," Julep said.

"Saying 'really' three times in a row doesn't do that much." Jo Bell sniffed. "You were insensitive. It was very immature of you, very pre-K."

This made Julep bristle. The greatest insult her older siblings could deliver was to call her "pre-K." She racked her brain to think of words, big words, that would say how sorry she felt.

"All right." She looked up at Fatty's ear, where Felix rested. "Felix, I feel extremely sorry for my unkind remarks."

How's that for a pre-K kid? she thought. *Take that, Jo Bell, you fathead.* "Actually, I so regret my behavior that I feel absolutely squishy in my spinnerets."

"Ick," Felix and Jo Bell said at the same time.

Julep thought she was on a roll and continued. "It was unfair of me to say 'no fair.' I apologize."

"Thank you, Julep. I accept your apology," Felix responded.

But the word "fair" stayed with Felix. Was it fair that he had to lead a hidden life just because of his species? Should he be judged by the venom in his fangs? There was so much more to him.

That's what isn't fair! he thought dolefully.

He winced as he remembered that his mom had said it was a crime to show himself. *How lame!* He felt a twinge where his leg had once been. But in her heart of hearts, did she really think he was so bad?

"Mom, there's something I —"

"Not now, Felix. Once we're settled."

Edith had turned a deaf ear to her children's squabbling. She was completely focused on where they should go and so grateful that Fat Cat had agreed to carry her wounded son. She knew that they could not travel far, but they had to get away. As soon as the paramedics saw the drops of blue blood, the pest control people would be called — the E-Men! There had been no time to clean up after themselves. The basement was filled with webs, rising like the vaporous mists of twilight. The blue tint of those webs was unique to brown recluses. A "dead giveaway," as Edith had once heard an E-Man exclaim with merriment. There was nothing worse than an exterminator who was a jokester.

The E-Men would also find the fresh flies that Edith had neatly bound up for their midnight supper. A supper she and her children would never be able to eat. And, of course, the exterminators would find Felix's leg. There had been no time to hide it.

Within minutes the word would go out — an infestation of *Loxosceles reclusa*, or brown recluse spiders, had been found at the philharmonic hall. And yet the Maestro was not a victim of her son's fangs. He'd fainted from the shock of seeing Felix. What might he have thought when he spotted the telltale

violin-shaped mark on Felix's head? Did he rec-
ognize the badge of the brown recluse? Or could
he guess that her shy son was not simply venomous but also deeply musical?

A sign appeared, hanging over a shop.

Fatty and Edith saw it at the same time. "Oh,
dear!" He sighed. Edith stopped. She floated out
a silk line and skibbled up to the ledge of the

display window to peer in. There were impressive accretions of dust.

Ah, yes! Edith spotted an orb weaver's web between the chin and neck of a ship's figurehead that was carved to look like an Indian princess. Edith didn't particularly care for orb weavers. They tended to be fussy. And they considered themselves vastly superior because of their fancy spiral-shaped webs. From the looks of it, this orb weaver was from a more ancient lineage than most.

However, these were desperate times. Felix needed to settle down and rest so he could molt.

Please, Edith silently prayed. *May Felix molt soon so his leg grows back!* If she could just keep him well fed and healthy, the chances for a quick molt were good.

The store was dusty, and there were droppings inside on the windowsill. There would be mice for Fatty. *Very good,* Edith thought.

Suspended from the ceiling in the middle of the store was a replica of the *Kon-Tiki* raft. The famed Norwegian explorer Thor Heyerdahl had used this raft to cross the Pacific. *This store is a hobby business for someone,* thought Edith. *The owner might only come in a few times a week. Perfect!*

The Kontiki Antikies shop offered many of the features that Edith always sought — dust, a hint of filth, and delightful clutter. But Edith worried that the contents of the shop were more like junky secondhand objects than genuine antiques. There was a whiff of the tacky to the shop. It reminded her of Tchotchkes Unlimited, a store in New York, where she and her late husband had spent their honeymoon in a plastic flamingo. They were so swept up in their young love that they hadn't noticed when their flamingo home was loaded onto a semitrailer truck. Before they could blink, they'd been shipped to Arizona with a half ton of other lawn ornaments.

Edith looked up at Kontiki Antikies and hoped it would prove to be a good temporary home. She sought peace and quiet, and though she was fond of filth, she also longed for a certain amount of culture and history. She yearned for a place where she could show her children the richness of history, all while hidden safely away. Life in the open was unthinkable.

She turned to her three children. "Come, I want to tell you what this shop might offer." She paused. "And, Felix, I would like you to come down from Fatty and try walking a bit."

"Really?" Felix asked.

"Yes, you don't want your remaining seven legs to weaken. They need a bit of exercise." She cleared her throat and tucked her fangs neatly beneath her chelicerae, the jaws she used for grasping food. "Now, listen up. Many years ago, before I was born —"

"Oh, wow, Mom, before you were born!" Jo Bell said.

"Totally ancient," Julep whispered.

"Not *that* ancient. But before I was born, a dashing adventurer named Thor Heyerdahl made a voyage across the vast Pacific Ocean. He wanted to prove that such routes could have been used by ancient people and that contact between South Amcrica and Polynesia was possible. It was a very daring feat."

"But, Mom," Felix said. "You always told us that many spiders came to America by floating across on flimsy logs and stuff. So it wasn't all that daring."

"Yes, but spiders are probably one-millionth the size of human beings. No great feat, really. And we didn't have to sail the craft, navigate. We just . . . just sort of . . ."

"Went with the wind, going with the flow," Jo Bell offered.

"Yes, more or less. But my point, children, is

that this shop appears to specialize in models of the original raft, the *Kon-Tiki*. And now, Fatty, we'll have to find an entrance for you."

Fatty sighed. "There's probably a cellar window in the back. I can squeeze in, I suppose."

"Look, Fatty," Edith said softly. "I know you don't have the fondest memories of the sea, given your history, but think of this as temporary. You can go back to your dear philharmonic hall in a few days, if you wish. By then the fumes will have cleared out. Or perhaps you could continue with us, once Felix grows a new leg. We could find a theater, a new one."

"Yes, yes, perhaps." For life without Edith and her children would be lonely for Fat Cat. There was too deep a bond between them. After all, he had carried that egg sac in his ear for almost a month. He was the godspider to her children. As the old saying went, "The show must go on!" but Fatty wasn't going anywhere.

FIVE
Kontiki Antikies

Not here!" a voice threaded through the dust that hung like vapor in the dim light of the shop. The voice came from the figurehead of the Indian princess in the display window. It was a handsomely carved lady with a profile designed to cut the wind and soft, almost kissable lips despite the fact that they were painted wood. Those lips had definitely not spoken the rude words that greeted their arrival.

"I might have known," Edith muttered. It was, of course, the master of the orb web. She could see him in a corner just above the web in a cottony sac.

"Don't worry," Edith called. "I'm sure we'll find a place far from your quarters." She looked

NOT HERE!

around somewhat doubt-
fully. The shop was
much smaller than she
had anticipated.

"We, my wife and I, would
be profoundly grateful. We rarely mix
with your kind. Little in common, you
know, and then our next batch is hatching
any day. We wouldn't want them getting the
wrong ideas."

"About what?" Julep stopped in her tiny
tracks. "What wrong ideas?"

"Never mind, Julep," Edith said quickly.
"Follow me."

"Ideas," muttered Felix, limping along behind
his mother. He suspected these spiders never
thought, let alone had ideas.

"I'm sure you understand," the voice said.

"We *are* the five-hundredth generation of our family. I am Oliphant Uxbridge. We can trace our family back to the *Mayflower*. Remarkable, isn't it? Our forebears came over in a crate of gunpowder."

For a spider who did not like to mix with their "kind," Edith thought he was awfully chatty. But she simply could not let the gunpowder remark pass. "Odd!" she said softly.

"Odd? What's odd? You don't believe that we came over on the *Mayflower* with the founders of this country?"

"Oh, no, not that. It is odd that the *Mayflower* humans, who came over for religious reasons, would have gunpowder. I don't associate such types with violence. Although I suppose they did become rather violent later on."

"How do you mean?"

"All that witchcraft business in Salem."

Oliphant Uxbridge seemed temporarily at a loss for words. "Are you an *intellectual*?" he said with sudden suspicion. "We don't particularly care for intellectuals. Radicals, the whole lot of them."

"I read," Edith said simply.

"Hrrumph," Oliphant grunted. "And what's wrong with that child — deformity?"

Edith gasped, but Felix replied before she could.

"I lost a leg, sir," he said with quiet dignity. "It is not a deformity."

Edith could hardly contain her rage. "There is no such thing as a deformity. There are only minds deformed by the wrong values. Felix is a special-needs child until he molts and grows a new leg." Her mind reeled back to countless humiliations she had suffered as a youngster, not because of anything she had ever done but merely because of the brown recluse reputation. Her father — with the best of intentions — had exposed them to too much. He was a bit of an adventurer. It was fine for humans like Thor Heyerdahl but not for brown recluse spiders. Life was so unsettled with adventurers.

"Don't engage them," his wife could be heard whispering. "They're brown recluses, and you know what that means! They've been outcasts for generations. No manners whatsoever. Very primitive."

Felix felt something contract within him. *So now being a recluse means we're ignorant!* But as they made their way toward a distant corner, Felix paused and turned to take one last look at the orb weaver's web. He hated to admit it, but its shimmering geometry entranced him.

Edith looked about, wondering where to lead her little family. The store was a hodgepodge. There were dust-encrusted compasses and navigational instruments, old sea charts, maps, globes, and hundreds upon hundreds of model ships, ranging from somewhat flimsy-looking rafts like the *Kon-Tiki* to more modern vessels. Clipper ships and yachts were all jumbled together. It wasn't like a library, where the books were properly ordered by subject matter and author. "Oh, mercy, one must bless the Dewey decimal system!" she whispered.

"What, Mom?" Jo Bell asked.

"Nothing, dear," Edith answered as she walked by another family of orb weavers who had spun a web in another figurehead. It seemed as if the orb weavers had staked out all the best figurehead real estate. She supposed her family was destined for the worst spot in the store. It was too bad. She had just passed by a large round table piled high with ship's lanterns, old dive helmets, and miniature cannons. *Felix would have loved to live in a cannon!*

"Pssst!" Fatty hissed from a corner. Edith and her two daughters scuttled over a pile of navigational charts to a far corner of the store.

"What have you found, Fatty?" Edith asked, and then her six eyes lit on her new home. "Oh, my word! Perfect."

There, perched on a pedestal, was a model of a square-rigged ship called the USS *Constitution*.

Above the ship, the model of the *Kon-Tiki* raft swung from the ceiling.

"Look, Mom!" said Felix. "You'll hardly have to weave a web. It's like it's already been done!"

"That's the rigging, dear. I doubt if it can compare in strength to what I spin . . . wouldn't trust it."

"Each of us kids can have a mast," said Jo Bell.

"Your mother should definitely get the captain's quarters aft of the wheel. They'll be the most luxurious," Fat Cat said.

"I think Felix should be there with me. I don't want him dangling about with only seven legs," Edith replied.

"Aw, Mom! I'll be fine. Look, I walked into the store, didn't I? Honestly, I think I might feel a molt coming on!" argued Felix.

"First things first," Edith said. "We have to go hunting. I don't know about the rest of you, but I'm starved. And, Fatty, I saw some mice droppings, so there's got to be a mouse for you around here somewhere."

"Don't worry, Edith. I've already had my appetizer course."

"My goodness, you don't waste any time."

"Ruled by my stomach too often, I fear. But I noticed some plump cockroaches by the cellar window as I pushed through."

"Yum!" Julep exclaimed. "Maybe there's some ketchup around."

"Oh, no, not the ketchup thing again," Jo Bell moaned. "Why would you think there would be ketchup here? It's an antique shop, not a school cafeteria." Ever since their mother had told them about lunch at the Martin Luther King Jr. Elementary School, Julep had been obsessed with ketchup.

"But don't cockroaches with ketchup sound so delicious?" Julep asked.

"Please, children, let's get settled," Edith said. *Why did I ever mention ketchup to this child? She never forgets a thing!*

SIX
Settling In

Edith had somewhat of a love-hate relationship with the word "settle." She liked to settle, she liked the feeling of being settled. But usually a horrible period of unsettlement came first. She had to admit that she had settled in the philharmonic hall for quite a long time. Her children had all hatched and spent their whole lives there. So she should not complain. By Julep's age, she and her family had moved half a dozen times.

She had seen more E-Men than she cared to remember. Her dear old aunt Tessie had finally said, "No more!" She squatted down in the deepest corner of her web and refused to budge. And she had, of course, been killed by the poison gas that jetted out of the white tanks the E-Men wore on their backs.

Edith's entire childhood had been lived on high alert. Her father seemed to thrive on this sort of excitement. Edith thought her mother did, too, until her father died. That was when her mother had begun talking about the Place Where Time Has Stopped. It wasn't just a place that promised peace and quiet and no fear of E-Men. It was also a place where brown recluses were never whispered about by other spiders.

Mrs. Uxbridge's remarks had cut deep. Her words brought back every bit of teasing Edith had endured as a child. She remembered in particular a period of time in an old barn in New England. There had been a lovely woodpile where her family had fetched up. All sorts of other spiders had strung their webs throughout the barn — orb weavers, sheet web weavers, jumping spiders, even leucauge spiders, a spider of stunning beauty, as dazzling as an Easter egg. In this barn, a young leucauge spider named

Barbie led a group of girls that operated like some sort of horrid children's militia. They called themselves "spiderniks," and their mission was to bully any newcomer, especially if that newcomer was a brown recluse. When Edith's mother complained, all Barbie's mother said was, "Rites of passage — it will teach her to be prepared."

"Prepared for what — cruelty? Mercy me, they call *us* deadly, but you, madam, are raising a little tyrant with Barbie."

Yes, Edith knew too well that the taunting words of other spiders could be as toxic as the chemicals in the E-Men's tanks. Such words could break your spirit. She had vowed she would never expose her own children to such viciousness. She would be the most reclusive of all recluses.

Although the shop was filled with spiders, the model ship would provide them with some isolation from the general spider population. Not only that, but this ship would offer a wonderful history lesson. The USS *Constitution* had distinguished itself in the War of 1812. Edith could not believe the lengths to which the model builders had gone to copy the original vessel. There were tiny, plush, red velvet cushions on the settees that edged the handsomely paneled captain's quarters. A navigation desk the size of a postage stamp had a set of navigation tools all made to scale: a tiny sextant used for measuring the angle of the sun or a star from the horizon, a ruler, a divider for measuring distances on a chart, and the chart itself. Hanging on the wall above the desk were even two miniature gleaming cutlasses.

Edith decided that first she would spin a web just over the settee, where a lovely set of fanlight windows curved so the captain could look out at the wake of his ship. She suspended herself mid-weaving to peer out and imagine an ocean with rolling waves cut by frothy foam from a ship under sail. Suddenly, a luminous green light flowed in through the windows.

"Oh, Fatty, isn't this cabin lovely!"

Fat Cat had hopped up onto the table where the ship model was perched and was peering through the stern windows.

"Yes. And although I have never had children, I do believe mothers need a little alone time," he said.

"Indeed!"

But just as Edith wove the last strand of her web, a voice piped up.

"Mom!"

"Felix! I thought you wanted to sleep topside, in the rigging."

"My leg hurts."

"It can't hurt." Jo Bell swung in on a thread of silk that she quickly anchored to one of the tassels on the plush pillows.

"What do you mean 'it can't hurt'?" Felix huffed.

"Your leg, in case you have forgotten, is back at the philharmonic!"

"Phantom pain," Fatty offered from the stern.

"You mean like a ghost?" Julep asked, crawling down from a hatch over the navigation table.

"And what are you doing here, Julep?" Edith asked.

"I didn't want to sleep up there all by myself."

"Not too near those cutlasses, Felix," Edith

cautioned. Although they were only models, they looked quite sharp.

"Julep, I thought you wanted to sleep in the lookout place, the crow's nest, at the top of the mast!" Jo Bell said. "Julep made this big deal about sleeping in it. And actually I was the one who had dibsed it."

"You did not!" Julep shot back.

"Did, too."

"Did not!"

"Did, too!"

"Did not!"

"Children! Children! Quit this squabbling," Edith commanded. "And, Felix, get that line you just floated *away* from the cutlasses." Then she muttered to herself, "So much for peace and quiet!"

The flashing lights of an ambulance swept through the storefront window. The family fell silent.

After a frozen minute, Jo Bell said, "They must be taking the Maestro away now."

"I hope he lives," Felix said with a sob threatening to burst like a small thundercloud. "He was so . . . so . . ."

"Gifted," Fatty finished the thought.

But Edith was not thinking about the Maestro at all. She was listening to the slow grind of the fire truck's gears as it turned around. Its siren was replaced by the shrill *waaaaa!* of an ambulance. The fire alarm was false, Edith thought, but how soon would the medics discover the *real* alarm — those tiny pale drops of blue, the blood of a spider, on the Maestro's cuff?

"Just a minute, children. I'll be right back." Edith used Julep's dragline to hoist herself on deck, then scuttled up the rigging to the crow's nest. Although the USS *Constitution* was on a table toward the back of the store, she had a clear view from her perch. Edith didn't have to wait long before she spotted the flash of the white truck and the blurred letters on its side. L.A. CHEMICAL. She felt a shiver pass through every hair on each of her eight legs. *They're always so discreet,* she thought with contempt. *They never advertise what they really do. Fearful of causing a panic, no doubt.* For what was more shameful than an infestation, particularly in a temple of art! And now the E-Men were arriving at the philharmonic hall with their poisons. Forget that fund-raising gala next week! They wouldn't be able to raise a penny for ages. *All because of us!* she thought mournfully.

The words rattled through her, right down to her spinnerets.

SEVEN
Webtime Stories

Felix felt awful, and it wasn't just his leg. He was haunted by his mom's words. "Felix's only crime was that he showed himself." He knew she didn't really think he was a criminal, but it still hurt. His mother was smart. There was no denying it. But if only she were more artistic. His mom always said that brown recluses were misunderstood. But Felix was misunderstood by his own mother! And there was a crime he was guilty of — causing his family to have to move. They were unsettled! A condition that Edith loathed with all her eight legs, six eyes, and every fiber of her body.

But while Felix was worrying about his mother, Edith was worrying about her son. He had been so quiet since he had arrived in her cabin. And she sensed that it was more than just his leg. She had caught him looking back at the orb weaver's web. He was one little knotted-up wad of silk.

"How about I tell you children a story?"

"Oh, yes!" they all cried, even Felix.

"Yes, Mom, tell us a story, please! I know it would make my leg feel better," Felix begged.

"Your late leg, which now resides in the philharmonic hall," Jo Bell said.

"Stop it, Jo Bell. Stop it this instant!" Edith snapped. Spiders cannot really snarl. Not exactly. But if they want to add an edge to their communications, they can send fierce vibrations through their webs. The children all shut up. A cross fire of glances shot among all three sets of eyes.

After several silent seconds, Felix ventured to speak. "A story would be nice, Mom."

Then Julep, in a very tiny voice, said,

"Maybe the one about the Place Where Time Has Stopped?"

"Oh, yes, I like that story," Fatty said. He was still perched on the table behind the aft cabin windows. The light from his eyes enveloped them all in a lovely green glow.

"All right, gather round, children." She paused. Edith never stayed angry for long. "Here, Felix, tuck in next to me, and Jo Bell, there's a nice pocket in the starboard corner for you and one to port for Julep."

"What's port? What's starboard?" Julep asked.

"Sailors' terms for left and right on a ship. Port is the left side when facing the front of a boat, starboard the right," Edith explained. "As long as we are on a ship, we might as well use the correct language."

Edith folded her fangs neatly and settled herself into the center of her lopsided web. Then she began speaking in that slow, reflective voice that the children called her webtime story voice. It was as if the voice traveled back through a dim, dusty web of time, the gauzy blue mists of "the so long ago." Human children might call these old stories fairy tales or legends or folktales. It was a time when stories that one wanted so desperately to believe really happened — just like the Place Where Time Has Stopped.

"There is a place far, far away. Some say it is a grand mansion, some say it is a small cabin in

the woods, some say it is across an ocean — but I don't think that's so." And Edith's three children would always repeat silently to themselves those last six words, for they gave them hope. "Nonetheless —" Edith's voice would now quicken. "There is a place where it is said that time has stopped.

"What does that mean, that time has stopped? Does it mean that there is only summer or only winter? That there is only one moment, which has been frozen into forever-ness? That is not what's most important about this place. For in this place, spiders are not feared. We are considered no more deadly than a daisy, less annoying than a mosquito. And we can live in peace and harmony. The E word is never mentioned.

"According to legend, the place was discovered by a wandering hobo spider, a funnel weaver who had escaped the great extermination. Hobo spiders are also feared because of their venom. But we are decidedly more toxic.

The hobo spiders arrived in this country, in the Pacific Northwest, long after we did."

She cast a glance toward the snobby orb weaver Oliphant Uxbridge. "But I am not going to get into a my-ancestors-came-earlier-than-yours-did competition. It doesn't matter where you came from or how long ago. It doesn't matter who you are in life but, rather, what you do. Remember that, children." Edith paused, and each one of her six eyes gleamed as she looked at her three children.

But it does matter, thought Felix. *Nobody likes us, just because of our venom.* The argument started again inside his head. But now was not the time. He wanted to hear this webtime story.

"In any case, this hobo spider was unfairly blamed for a lot of 'attacks' on humans. The bites were not fatal, and the hobo spider was not at fault. Nonetheless, the word was out and a wide extermination was launched to rid three states of these hobo spiders — Oregon, Washington, and Idaho. Only a few spiders survived. And there was one who was said to have left the Northwest for a place far, far away. Some say he caught a ride on a freighter to Japan. Others claim that he went north, into the Arctic with the ice spiders."

"It would stop time if he was frozen," Felix offered.

"The spider traveled alone, nameless, anonymous. You see, this hobo's bite had been mistaken for our bite, a brown recluse bite. He wanted nothing to do with any spiders after that. He sought solitude."

"Does that mean he doesn't like us?" Julep asked mournfully.

"It only means that he likes being alone better than keeping company," Edith answered. "As the story goes, the hobo's bites in the Place Where Time Has Stopped made the humans there even stronger and less fearful of all spiders. It is said that venom runs in their blood."

"Did he bite them on purpose or accidentally?" Felix asked.

"I don't know," Edith said softly. "I simply do not know."

"Is this story really true, Mom?" Julep asked.

"I don't know," she said again. "But even if it isn't true, it's so lovely to think about. So peaceful. So . . . so . . . settled."

EIGHT
Cause for Celebration

And it was said that my four-times-squared great-grandmother, Old Number Sixteen as we called her, occupied the cabin of John Carver, the first governor of the Plymouth Colony, and — listen to this, dear — was present at the signing of the Mayflower Compact!"

"Oh, Oliphant! I never tire of this story."

"Well, guess what? We do!" Jo Bell muttered.

It was their second night in the store. The good news was that the owner had not yet shown up, so Edith felt sure that Kontiki Antikies was a hobby business for someone. The bad news was that Oliphant Uxbridge loved droning on about his family day and night.

"I wish he'd shut up already. If I have to hear
one more story about his stupid *Mayflower*
ancestors, I'm going to —" Felix groaned.

"Children, it's time for sleep," Edith said. But
it was hopeless. Despite the fact that they were
at the back of the shop and nowhere near the
Uxbridges' web, Oliphant's voice carried.

"How can we, Mom, with him droning on?"
Jo Bell sighed.

"Get used to it!" called a voice. It was coming from a neighboring ship, a lovely model of
the famous clipper *Cutty Sark.*

"Who's that?" Edith called cautiously. She

knew there were other spiders about, but no one had spoken to them except the Uxbridges. Their privacy had been respected, or perhaps their presence was dreaded. Still, Edith had been happy to be left alone.

"Doris," came the reply.

"What are you?"

"Black widow."

Edith felt a small twinge of relief. At least it was not another orb weaver, and Doris was toxic, too.

"I know what you're thinking!" Doris said in a somewhat unpleasant voice.

"How could you possibly know what I am thinking?" Edith asked.

"I wasn't hatched yesterday, dearie. I've been around your kind."

Edith did not like her tone at all. *Your kind! How rude!*

Doris continued, "Believe me, you are just as toxic as I am."

"Then you should understand!"

"Ha!" The rigging vibrated with the harsh laugh.

"Mom," Felix implored. "Why don't you tell her off? Why didn't you say, 'Hey, Miss Smarty Legs, at least we don't murder our mates and eat them!'"

"Let her be, Felix. Just let her be."

Edith decided that silence was the best strategy with her new neighbor. She had met too many of Doris's "kind" before. The greater population of black widows was so insecure they had to pick on someone they considered beneath them — usually their mates or a creature more toxic. Edith was always hoping to encounter a black widow pair like the couple she and her husband had met at Tchotchkes Unlimited in Brooklyn. Now, there was a couple of good souls. Albert and Rachel — the two were on their honeymoon as well, and they were determined to buck the current. Rachel point-blank refused to kill her mate. "Tough spinnerets!" she huffed. "This one's a keeper. I'm not letting him go!"

When the first gray threads of dawn wove through the darkness of the store, the family was still asleep, except for Felix. The night before, he had noticed a newsstand just outside the shop. He knew the morning edition of the *Los Angeles Times* was delivered very early, and he planned to be on the windowsill to see if there was a story about the philharmonic hall. Like most spiders, Felix's distance vision was not great. The world out there was generally fuzzy, despite his six eyes. But he could see these headlines all too well! Big black block letters seemed to roar:

INFESTATION OF DEADLY SPIDERS
IN PHILHARMONIC HALL
Conductor Found Collapsed!

Oh, no! Felix silently groaned. There seemed to be a drawing of a brown recluse on the front page. Beneath it were the words "If you see this spider, contact pest control immediately. Call 1-800-EEK-PEST."

"I'm wanted!" Felix muttered. He strained to see, but he couldn't read anything else from the windowsill. It was profoundly frustrating. Did the conductor live or die?

Felix returned to the captain's quarters of the USS *Constitution*. His family was still asleep, but try as he might, Felix couldn't join them.

Over the next few days, Edith and her children became accustomed to the endless blathering of Oliphant Uxbridge and the pace of life in the antique store. Countless times a day, Felix announced that a molt was coming on. But Edith knew it would be a while and cautioned him to be patient.

Then one morning a week after their arrival, she heard a scuttling in the rigging. Felix swung in on a silk thread through a porthole. "Ta-da!" he announced.

"What's all the ta-da-ing about?" Jo Bell asked as she trussed up a carpenter ant.

Edith looked hard at her son. She took a tiny step closer and focused all of her eyes. Her minuscule heart skipped a beat. "Felix! Your leg! You have a new leg!"

NINE
Attack!

"Could you keep it down!" The merry little spider family froze. They were gathered around a large cockroach, celebrating Felix's new leg. Through small puncture wounds made by her fangs, Edith had delivered the first stunning doses of her venom. The cockroach was barely stirring now. Each member of Edith's family was preparing to vomit a bit of their own digestive fluids in through the puncture wounds so the guts of the cockroach would liquefy and could be sucked out.

"You know what would taste great with this? Ketchup!"

"Julep, stop already!" Jo Bell rolled her eyes.

Oliphant Uxbridge's complaint cut through the little party. "I say, you've been carousing about this molt and your son's newly grown leg for hours now. I believe our egg sac is showing signs of hatching. I would appreciate it if our spiderlings could hatch into a more refined environment."

"Just wait until one of them loses a leg. You'd be celebrating, too!" Felix blurted out.

"Felix!" Edith hissed.

"Well, it's true, Mom," he muttered.

They heard a painful wail from Mrs. Uxbridge. "Oliphant, that family is so vulgar. Don't even speak to them. You know nothing ever good happens when brown recluses move into the neighborhood. Why, I heard sirens out there the very night they arrived. I bet anything it was something to do with *them*. Brown recluses — they give us all a bad name!"

Fear coursed through Edith. Mrs. Uxbridge had made the connection between Edith's family and the sirens. A sense of defeat engulfed her. Fat Cat, however, had heard enough. Arching his back in anger, he sprang across the shop to where the Uxbridges' web hung in all its spiraling delicacy.

"How dare you speak that way to my dear friend! 'Vulgar,' you call her! My dear madame, you wouldn't know vulgar if it smacked you in the face." Fat Cat was in full voice now. Edith and her children clambered up the USS *Constitution*'s rigging to watch Fat Cat's performance. Scores of other spiders in the shop began creeping out from their webs. A leucauge family appeared from a dented globe. Another black widow emerged from a chronometer. A pholcid descended from a shelf of compasses for a better view. Fatty was thrilled with his arachnid audience and puffed up to deliver his speech.

"You have a tiny mind, fitted with ordinary thoughts and downright meanness! You know nothing except your own dismal little ancestral history," the cat cried out.

"Here! Here! I take offense," Oliphant Uxbridge fumed.

"You give offense, sir!" Fat Cat replied.

There was nothing more satisfying for Edith than seeing the pompous spider taken down a notch. It was as delicious as a tasty cockroach. But beneath the fizz and sizzle of the argument, Edith began to detect a dimmer set of vibrations. What were they? From one of her six eyes she noticed a glistening thread floating softly toward where she perched in the rigging.

My goodness — a courtship thread! Oh, I'm

much too old. A widow with three kids. Then it struck her. The single word formed in her mind, each letter dropping slowly into place. M-I-M-E-T-I-D-A-E — pirate spiders!

It was an attack.

"NO!" she screamed. "Abandon ship!"

The pirate spiders used an old ruse. Send out a courtship thread, reel the victim in, and then with one quick bite to the leg, in goes the poison and . . .

Edith couldn't bear the thought. Felix had just grown a new leg!

Pirates were one of the few spiders Edith knew, aside from black widows, who specialized in killing their own. How cunning they had been in their mimicry of brown recluse vibrations. They had obviously been in the store the entire time. Most likely they had been hiding out on the *Kon-Tiki* raft that hung above the *Constitution.*

"Get out, kids! Get out! Pirates!" Edith yelled.

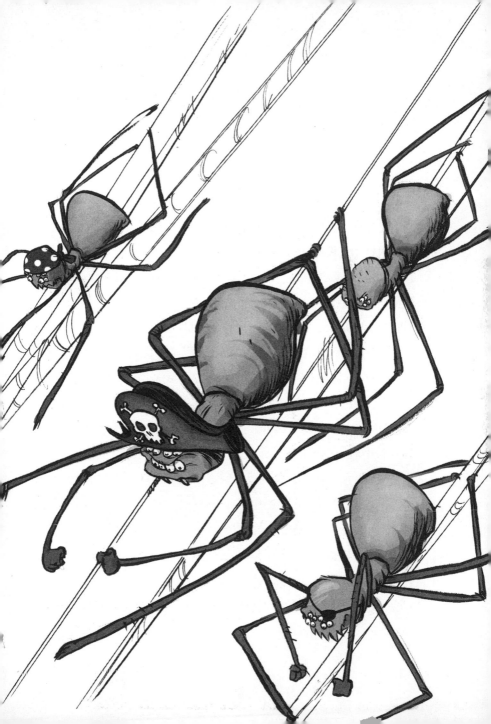

She could now see the distinctive spinelike hairs that lined the long front legs of the pirate spiders. Four pirates crawled onto the deck and up the rigging after Julep and Jo Bell, who scuttled toward the crow's nest. Felix was on the foredeck. *They'll be trapped!*

Edith looked around wildly, but her son had disappeared. "Felix, where are you? Felix!" she screamed.

Fat Cat bounded over, teeth bared.

"Don't get near them!" Edith shouted. "They're almost as toxic as we are!"

Suddenly, there was a glittering flash from the mizzenmast. It was Felix swinging by his fresh new leg. In his forward appendages, his pedipalps, he grasped the miniature cutlasses.

"Felix!" Edith exclaimed.

"Mom, catch this!"

The curved blade sailed toward her on a high quality, number one grade silk thread. It was catch or be killed! But Felix's aim was perfect. Edith caught the cutlass and slashed the so-called "courtship thread." Felix quickly suspended himself over the nearest pirate. With a quick flick of the cutlass, he separated the spider's head from its body. "Bye-bye," he said as the spider's head tumbled to the deck.

The other three spiders were stunned. Then they began to argue.

"He said it would work!"

"He said it always worked!"

Unnoticed by the arguing spiders, Edith scuttled up the ratlines, the small ropes between the shrouds of the mast. She sliced off another pirate head.

"Go, Mom!" Felix yelled.

"No, *they're* going! After them!" she cried.

This attack was definitely planned. Edith realized that the pirates had worked to create a highway of silk toward the front of the store. They were headed that way — straight toward the Uxbridges. Seconds later, there was a shriek from the figurehead. "My babies! My babies!" It was Mrs. Uxbridge.

The two remaining pirate spiders were climbing up the lovely neck of the figurehead toward Mrs. Uxbridge.

"Your wife or the egg sac — what'll it be?"

TEN

Turmoil in the Uxbridge Web

Now, shouldn't we discuss this as civilized spiders?" Oliphant Uxbridge replied. His voice sounded unnaturally calm.

The two pirates started to laugh. "Who said anything about civilized!" one said. He moved toward Oliphant, waving his spine-studded front legs. "Keep watch on the missus, Seven Eyes."

"You bet, Cap," Seven Eyes replied. The second pirate was missing an eye. Unlike brown recluses, pirate spiders had eight eyes, arranged in two rows.

Edith and Felix had suspended themselves from a dust-encrusted ship's lantern opposite the figurehead. The egg sac glimmered softly in the reflection of the streetlight outside. *This is terrible,* Edith thought. *A hundred innocent lives cut off!*

She and Felix exchanged glances, a cross fire of desperate looks from their dozen eyes. They were not in a good place to attack. Oliphant Uxbridge would be no help. His wife was growing hysterical as he continued to converse.

"Oliphant! He's coming closer to the sac! Oliphant, do something!"

"I think we could make an arrangement of some sort. My wife, she is lovely, I admit. But, well . . . I guess I could find anoth —"

"Are you nuts?" Edith screamed. "You lousy good-for-nothing!"

At that moment, there was another tiny glimmer above the ship's figurehead.

"Hi, guys!" said Julep.

Edith was stunned. How in the name of silk and venom had her daughters gotten there so quickly? But there they were! The two girls were swinging from silken threads attached to a block and tackle used for hoisting sails.

"Ahoy there!" cried Jo Bell, wiggling a dragline.

The two pirates launched themselves toward the sisters. But blinded by the streetlight outside, they had not seen the kill trap that Julep and Jo Bell had spun. They were caught! Julep and Jo Bell perched in opposite corners of the kill trap, paying out binding silk as fast as they could.

"Make it tight. Steer clear of their fangs, girls." Edith paused to look at her three children in awe. "Brilliant, just brilliant," she murmured.

"Thank you!" Mrs. Uxbridge gasped. "I don't know how to thank you. Your courage, your kindness."

"Yes, we cannot thank you enough," Oliphant chimed in.

Mrs. Uxbridge swung herself toward her husband and glared.

"What do you mean WE! You mealy-fanged, gutless, pompous ass. As soon as the eggs hatch, I'm out of here. And you get out now, on the double. Find yourself another figurehead to spin a web in. And find yourself another mate, as you suggested when you were about to hand me over to those thugs!"

"You can't mean it, dearest."

"I *do* mean it, and don't dearest me."

Fat Cat meowed, "Bravo, madame!"

"Mrs. Uxbridge, you are welcome to move onto the *Constitution* with us," Edith said.

"My dear, don't you want to reconsider?" Oliphant persisted.

"No, Oliphant. I don't. But I do owe Mrs. . . . what is your name?"

"Edith, just call me Edith."

"I do owe you an apology, Edith. You are not vulgar at all. And you may call me by my first name — Glory."

"Oh, my! My!" Edith murmured to no one in particular. "Let's go back and get settled. It's been quite a night."

Julep, Felix, and Jo Bell exchanged glances. The S word again. Whenever Edith said the word "settled," they knew she was anything but. However, they followed their mother back to the *Constitution.*

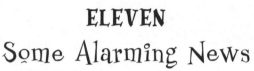

ELEVEN

Some Alarming News

Despite Edith's worries, life was settled for a while. Oliphant Uxbridge moved to another ship's figurehead. He lost no time in taking up with another orb weaver. Glory's egg sac hatched, but unfortunately the proprietor of the store left the door wide open on the very day the spiderlings arrived. A fresh breeze swept into the shop and all one hundred twenty-two little Uxbridges blew away, out of the shop and onto the winds to find their own way in the world. Glory was very upset and often dropped in to visit Edith.

"Imagine losing a husband and one hundred twenty-two children all within such a short time." Edith shook her head in sympathy. "But I know I'm better off without him. I do miss the

spiderlings, though. I hardly got to know them before that fool owner opened the doors. How would he like it if someone decided to air out the place where he lived and all his babies were swept away!" To emphasize her feelings, Glory plucked the filament from which she suspended herself through the hatch into Edith's cabin. Her visits were brief, and she never accepted an invitation to settle into the web for a nice long chat. She seemed to prefer rappelling down through the hatch and hanging on the end of the silk thread for a bit.

"Well, humans usually just have one child at a time, sometimes two or three. But never one hundred twenty-two," Edith offered.

"It doesn't matter — one or one hundred. You miss them all the same."

"Yes, I suppose so."

What worried Edith more than Glory Uxbridge's sadness over her spiderlings was the shopkeeper's sudden interest in cleaning. It did not bode well. Edith preferred a certain amount of dust, clutter, and downright filth. It was never a good sign when humans became too particular about housekeeping. She began having a vague premonition that she and her children were on the brink of another move. It was this fear that caused her to seek out a globe, not the dented globe where the leucauge spiders lived but one in better shape.

"Follow me, children. I want to show you the precise spot where the *Constitution* encountered the HMS *Cyane* and the HMS *Levant* in the War of 1812."

"But we know that," said Felix, resting on the chart in the cabin. "You showed us, remember?"

"Oh, yes, I did," Edith answered. "Well, how about I show you where the *Constitution* is right now?"

"It's still around after all these centuries?" Jo Bell asked.

"Absolutely!"

"You mean the real ship and not a model?" Felix asked.

"Positively." An idea, like the tiniest little flicker, began to glow in Edith's mind — *Boston!*

"Boston!" She blurted out the name of the old city where she had once lived with her mother after her father had died.

"Boston?"

"Yes, Boston! What a fine old city it is. Come quickly."

"To Boston?" Julep asked.

"No, to the globe so you can see it."

Two minutes later, Edith began to release some silk from the very tippy top of the globe. It was what her children called a "speaking thread." She suspended herself over the Arctic land mass and then rappelled down over the North Atlantic. At the fiftieth latitude, she swung east toward the coast of Newfoundland, continued her descent over Nova Scotia, Maine, and New Hampshire, and fetched up above the state of Massachusetts. To be exact, for Edith was a precise sort, her position was 42° north and 71° west, the latitude and longitude of the city of Boston.

"All eyes on me, please," she said.

Her three children, gathered near the Arctic Circle, looked down.

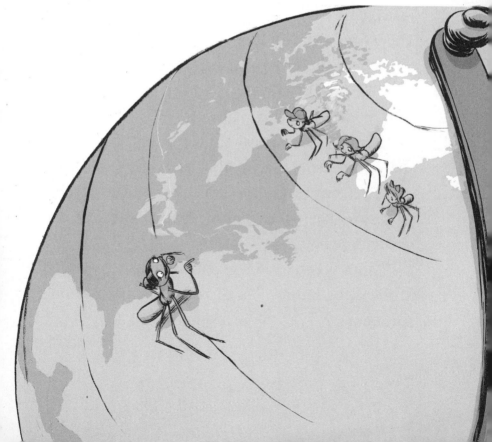

"I am dangling right above the coastline of the New England state of Massachusetts. This is Boston, home of the finest and the oldest public library in America! As I told you, my mother and I spent a very happy time there."

"But the E-Men came, right?" Jo Bell asked with a sigh.

"No, no."

"Then why did you leave?" Felix asked. There were several endless seconds, or so it seemed to the children, when Edith grew very still. "Well, Boston was where your grandma died, and I . . . I felt . . . so . . . so . . . ."

"Lonely?" Julep asked, thinking how lonely she would feel if her mother were gone.

"Yes, there were too many reminders, I suppose. We passed so many happy hours in the children's room."

"Mom," Felix said when they had returned to the *Constitution*. "Is there any art in Boston? Any music?"

"Yes, dear. A wonderful symphony orchestra, and the Museum of Fine Arts and the library. The library has magnificent murals."

"Hmm," Felix said. He glanced quickly over at the Uxbridges' web, in all its spiraling glory.

TWELVE
An Unblessed Event

Edith's fears of being unsettled became real one afternoon when Glory came to visit. It was an odd time of day for Glory to stop in, and as soon as she dropped through the hatch, Edith knew it was bad news.

"Don't tell me. He's cleaning again, right?" Edith asked.

"Worse."

"E-Men!"

Glory nodded.

"No!" Edith gasped. She took a deep breath and tried to compose herself. "Run that by me one more time, Glory. What were the owner's exact words?"

"The owner was on the telephone and said,

'My wife and I are having a baby, a blessed event. We've decided to sell the store, but we really have to clean it up.' Then he paused for almost a minute while I suppose the person on the other end said something. And then he said, 'Yes, we know about the brown recluses at the philharmonic and we realize they might be throughout the neighborhood.' Then he said, 'Yes . . . yes.' And then there was a part I didn't quite understand, something about 'so you have to tent the store.'"

"Tent the store! Oh, mercy! That's the worst!" Edith exclaimed.

"What does it mean, Mom?" Jo Bell asked. Every hair on her eight legs began to tremble.

"It basically means that they are going to suffocate us. It's the most complete form of extermination. We have to get out of here fast! We must sound the alarm for every creature in this place. Fatty, get over to that ship bell and start slamming the clapper. An announcement must be made or we'll all die. Then get ready because we're going now. This is a real catastrophe!"

"It is a most *un*blessed event!" Fatty replied. "Let's get the show on the road!" He leaped to the ship's bell and began ringing it.

"The road to where?" Jo Bell asked.

Felix and his mom looked at each other, a dozen eyes between them all picturing one place. "Boston!" they both said at once.

"But how will we get there?" Julep asked. "It's the other side of the country."

"Bus!" Fat Cat said. "There's a bus stop at the corner. If we switch at Sunset and Vine, we can catch a number four, ride it to the end of the line, and get to the terminal for buses headed cross-country."

"Fatty, you're a genius!" Edith exclaimed.

"Not at all. Just a well-traveled old theater cat. I know transportation — from my days with a traveling Shakespeare company."

* * *

Minutes later they were standing on the corner of Yucca and Las Palmas Avenue. Glory Uxbridge was perched on top of a fire hydrant and had begun to pay out the first of several silk threads. These lines were made of balloon silk, a special type of silk that gets caught by the wind. The spider would rise into the sky like a tiny kite.

"Before I pay out any more silk, I want to thank you all. In this breeze, I'll be off before you can flick a fang." She paused and looked up. "Look who's leaving now." She waved one leg toward a streetlight, at Oliphant and his new mate.

There were hundreds of orb weavers, more than Edith had ever imagined lived in the shop. Sunlight caught the spiders' silken threads, turning them a bright, shimmering gold. For a brief minute, it seemed as if a golden canopy were suspended over them. Edith and her children looked up in awe at the sight.

"Radiant!" Felix whispered. "Absolutely radiant!"

"Mom, why don't we balloon?" Julep whined as she watched Glory rise softly on the billows of wind.

"Hush, Julep. Here comes a bus. Okay, I want you all to line up next to me, and when the bus stops, just swing up. But don't go by the stairs — you might get squished. Get ready to cast a line and hoist yourself."

"I have a better idea," Fat Cat said. "All of you get on my back and I'll climb up on the rear fender."

"You're sure, Fatty? You're sure you can jump that high?"

"It's not that high. I am a veteran bus rider."

Fat Cat was as good as his word. They were soon all aboard the bus. Minutes later, as they rounded the corner on Yucca and Highland, Jo Bell called back to them with wonderful news. "Hey, he's back!"

"Who?" Edith called up.

"Leon Brinsky, the conductor. He survived! There's a big sign welcoming him back."

"Now, *that* is a blessed event!" Felix sighed with relief.

"I hope Felix will be exonerated," Edith called back up.

"What's exonerated?" asked Julep.

"Not blamed."

"What does it matter, if my musical career is finished?" Felix sighed.

"Not necessarily, dear. There is more music out there. Remember, we're going to Boston. There is music and art in Boston."

"But we're going to the library and not a symphony hall."

"Well, we'll see."

Felix hated it when his mother said "we'll see." Even worse was "we'll think about it." Because all she really ever wanted to see or think about was a dimmer, darker, more remote place to hide.

And a hidey-hole was exactly where Edith's musings were taking her. Someday, she thought, they would find everything they ever needed and wanted. And the Boston Public Library was a vast and wonderful place to start. She had left because she could not bear to be there without her mother. But now she had children of her own. If she were ever to find clues to the Place Where Time Has Stopped, it would be in the soft glow of those reading rooms filled with thousands upon thousands of books. There was so much to be explored, so much to read. And so many lovely places to hide.

THIRTEEN
Luxo Liner

After they had boarded the bus, Felix cast a line to the roof and skibbled off to explore. He was back in a few minutes.

"Hey, you should see what's on the side of this bus," Felix called out.

"What is it?" Jo Bell asked.

"It's an ad for a movie — about spiders!" Julep and Jo Bell scurried over to have a look. There was an advertisement running the length of the bus that showed an enormous spider with fangs the size of dinosaur teeth fighting a brawny man with a safari hat and a long whip.

"What in the name of venom does that fool think he's doing — a whip? Like a whip is going to help him. Why doesn't he just have a fumigation tank like other E-Men?" Jo Bell exclaimed.

"He's trying to be a hero," Felix said. "Movie heroes have whips, not fumigation tanks."

"That's not even a real spider! Look how they messed up his eyes!"

"Well, that's Hollywood for you!" Felix said.

"He is kind of handsome," Julep mused. "The man, that is."

"He looks like a jerk to me," Felix replied.

"What's the movie called?" Julep asked as the bus pulled up at a stoplight.

"'*Kentucky Jones and the Spiders of Doom,'*" Jo Belle said, reading upside down.

*   *   *

After another hour of riding, they arrived at the terminal. Edith immediately spotted a sign flashing BOSTON on a silvery blue bus, but Fatty was quick to redirect her.

"Not the Blue Fox line — no, never!"

"Why ever not?" Edith asked.

"You don't want to have to hang out in the lavatories all the time." He wrinkled his nose.

Edith knew that cats tended to be more sensitive than spiders about such things and gave Fatty a look.

"Edith, it's not only that!" he exclaimed. "It could be dangerous."

"Oh, yes, flushed away! Not like an outhouse. Outhouses can be very peaceful places," Edith said, recalling a favorite outhouse from her early childhood in Indiana. "So, what would you suggest, Fatty?"

"The Luxo Liner. Lovely reclining leather seats."

"We don't really require that," Edith said.

But Fat Cat explained that just any old bus to

Boston wouldn't do. "We must be sure to get aboard a Luxo Liner. First class the whole way. All the amenities, and amenities means plenty of nooks and crannies. Worktables for busy executives, Internet connections, outlets for laptops, a bar."

"We don't drink!" Edith exclaimed.

Fatty sighed. "Honestly, Edith. Don't you see — if there is a bar, there are shelves, cubbyholes for glasses and wine bottles."

Edith's six eyes shined brighter. "Now I'm getting it!"

"Yes! Nooks and crannies!" Fatty repeated.

Three hours later, Edith, her children, and Fatty were aboard the Luxo Liner heading east. It was all that Fatty had promised. Nooks and crannies galore. There were even movies!

FOURTEEN
A Myth In the Making?

There was the crack of a whip, then the sound of a Chinese gong. A rugged man wearing a safari hat appeared on the small screen. "Had a bit of a problem, ma'am?" A beautiful woman stepped forward.

"Trouble?" she asked.

"Someone put a spider where it isn't supposed to be." The camera came in for a close-up on the face of Kentucky Jones, famous arachnologist and treasure hunter.

Edith suspended herself from a reading light above the screen. "Jo Bell, Julep! I cannot believe you are watching this trash!" The two sisters were perched on the frizzy hair of a young woman whose eyes had been glued to the screen showing *Kentucky Jones and the Spiders of Doom*. "Even that stupid girl has fallen asleep."

"Great!" Jo Bell said. "I'm going to crawl in her ear so I can hear better through the headphones."

"It's not boring, Mom," Julep said. "The guy is such an idiot."

Jo Bell popped back out. "You can't believe what Kentucky Jones just said to his girlfriend!"

"What?" Julep asked.

"Get this — 'I would swim through an ocean of venom for you, sweetheart.' Ocean of venom — is that hysterical or what?"

Edith sighed. "Why don't you watch something with more educational value? Four rows up, there's a wonderful educational program about global warming."

"Booorrring!" both girls said at once.

"Global warming is a real problem, girls. It could threaten all our lives, the very existence of our species."

"Mom," Jo Bell said with a note of exasperation in her voice. "You're the one who's always telling us that spiders have been around forever, four hundred million years, much longer than humans. What's a little heat? I'm sure we'll survive."

Edith sighed. She wasn't going to push it. It was a long bus ride. She supposed it wouldn't hurt the children to watch an idiot actor gallivanting about. "Where's Felix? Why isn't he watching?"

"He's in the lavatory."

"That's dangerous!" Edith replied.

"No," Jo Bell said. "He's not *in* the toilet. He's just hanging out in a cabinet where they keep extra paper towels and stuff."

"Oh, dear, I better go check. Fatty sends his love from baggage."

Edith skibbled off to the lavatory. A woman was just pulling up her underpants as she arrived. Edith heard the roar of the toilet's flush and trembled. She certainly hoped Felix was where the girls had said. As the woman washed her hands, Edith crept up her skirt hem and then floated a line in toward the handle of the cabinet.

"Felix, are you in there?"

"Yeah, Mom. Wait until you see what I've done!"

"Oh, dear!"

"No, it's great. Come on in. You can squeeze through the crack."

Edith entered the shadowy space. The cabinet was large and half the paper towels had been used, so there was plenty of space. And now, strung between the remaining rolls, a glistening fragile geometry quivered in the dim light.

"Felix! Felix!" Edith was stunned. "What have you done?" *What have you become?* she thought in anguish, *an orb weaver?*

"I figured it out, Mom! It's amazing. I floated a line from that screw at the top and then another from the opposite side. Then I dropped a line from the center so it makes a kind of Y shape. But the hardest part was this crossband section in the middle. I used a combination of number one silk with number four. I know what you're thinking — odd combination of silk."

He has no idea what I am thinking! Edith made a small gasping noise, then plucked a thread with one of her legs to add vibrational emphasis to what she was about to say.

"It is not the oddness of the combination that startles me." She paused. "It's your oddness. You're acting like Oliphant Uxbridge!"

At least five of Felix's eight legs began to wobble as his mother spoke. "Mom." There was such anguish in his voice that Edith immediately knew she had gone too far. "Mom, I am NOT Oliphant Uxbridge. Not by any stretch of the imagination."

"I know that, dear."

"Then why did you say it, Mom? It's just like when we were back at the philharmonic and you said my only crime was —"

"But I said I misspoke."

"Did you, Mom, or did you really believe it? You act like not hiding out really is a crime. You have to loosen up!"

"I am loose," Edith protested. "That's why our webs are nice, cozy tangled affairs. This . . . this . . . is all too rigid, too inflexible, just like Oliphant Uxbridge!"

But Felix wouldn't back down. "You cannot judge spiders simply by their webs. It's not fair!"

Something flinched deep in Edith's spinnerets. There was truth to what her son was saying.

"I really miss the philharmonic," he continued. "I am an artist. I thought I was going to be a musician." He stopped. "I can't explain it, but I have these . . . these feelings . . . impulses for art. I need an outlet for them. What we weave is very practical, but am I destined to weave only gauzy, funny-shaped webs?"

"They're not funny-shaped!"

"All right, but they don't have the spiraling mystery of an orb web, the geometry. The beauty."

He was right, of course. The web he had woven was undeniably beautiful. However, to Edith it did not look natural. She shifted nervously on her rear four legs.

"Not everything has to be useful, Mom. I mean, it is useful — the capture spiral works for them. I can't wait to see if I trap anything."

"Hmmm" was Edith's only response.

At that moment Jo Bell and Julep arrived. "Holy silk, look at that, will you!" Jo Bell exclaimed.

"I thought you two were watching the movie," Edith said.

"It got boring," Julep replied. "Wow, Felix, what have you woven?"

"Spectacular, isn't it?" Felix was quivering with excitement now.

"It's simply the most beautiful web I've ever seen! I can't believe you did this all by yourself! Did you help him, Mom?" Julep turned to Edith.

"Certainly not! I am not an orb weaver. I wouldn't know where to begin."

"But neither is Felix!" Julep said.

"He's an artist!" Jo Bell added.

Felix seemed to swell with pride.

"Look at those graceful curves, that soaring funnel — all the geometric shapes. It's not simply flat like any old orb weaver web at all," Jo Bell continued.

"Oh, I wish that old windbag Oliphant Uxbridge could just see this," Jo Bell gushed. She turned to her mother. "Don't you, Mom?"

Edith was not so sure. The web was truly a shimmering construction — like nothing she had ever seen. There were shapes that swooped like rolling ocean waves, some that folded in on themselves, and others that arced and soared. Edith had to admit that her son had brought together all of his talents to create a symphony in silk!

It frightened her. For if anyone saw this — any human — it would draw attention. And attention from the human world could be fatal. She wasn't sure how to handle this. But the next words from Felix gave her an idea.

"I'd show that stuck-up old spider a thing or two about weaving," Felix proclaimed.

Edith found this comment worrying. She detected a whiff of pride in her son. He was a bright lad. But pride led to showing off. And that was the risk of Felix's artistic instincts. To express himself, he had to show himself. Art had too many occupational hazards.

"Children." She spoke very soberly.

"Yeah, Mom?" they all said at once.

"I think it's time for a webtime story."

"Oh, yay!" both Jo Bell and Julep cried. "We haven't had one in so long."

But Felix remained silent.

"Where will we go, your web or here?" Felix asked.

"Here, of course. This is a lovely web. I think it might be very nice for storytelling. You can all perch on one of those . . . those . . . what do you call those threads that make up the circles, dear?" Edith asked, turning to Felix.

"Spirals," he said quietly.

"So, what's the story, Mom?" Julep asked.

"This story is a myth," Edith replied.

"I love myths!" Julep bounced on her radial.

"Take it easy, Julep. I'm not sure how strong that is," Felix warned.

Edith continued. "The character in this myth is a girl and her name is Arachne."

"Arachne?" all three children asked at once.

"But that's what we're called. Spiders — arachnids," Jo Bell said. "So it's about a spider girl?"

"No, it's about a human girl."

"That can't be!" Jo Bell said. "Why would a human have a spidery name?"

"Because she was turned into a spider," Edith replied.

"SHE WHAT??!!" the three children of Edith all screamed at the same time.

FIFTEEN
Spider Girl

Edith had her children's undivided attention now. "Once upon a time, a very long time ago, Athena, the goddess of wisdom, heard about a young peasant girl named Arachne. Athena was known for her artistry and was a very fine weaver. Arachne also wove, and she boasted that she could make tapestries more beautiful than any god's or goddess's, even Athena's. Now, the gods and goddesses did not like it when anyone was compared to them. They were very proud."

"They had pride?" Julep asked.

"Yes, excessive pride," Edith replied with a nod. "And that was fine for gods and goddesses, but if humans showed excessive pride, it led to nothing but trouble. Gods and goddesses were jealous types."

Felix was still quiet but listening intently. "So, what happened?" he asked.

"Athena descended from her lofty perch on Mount Olympus," Edith continued. "She went to visit Arachne while disguised as an old lady. She told Arachne her work was beautiful but asked why she would ever compare herself to a goddess. Wasn't she happy to be the best weaver among the humans on earth?

"The girl, who was so prideful, answered her back, 'Let the goddess come! We'll have a contest and see who's the best!'"

"She sassed her!" Julep said. "She sassed a goddess!"

"Indeed she did!" Edith nodded.

"So, what happened next?" Felix asked suspiciously.

"Well, Athena grew furious and threw off her disguise. Standing before Arachne in all her goddess glory, she shouted, 'Prideful girl, you shall have your wish.' And so they sat down in front of two looms. Athena's tapestry was one of shimmering beauty and elegance. But so was Arachne's. However, what Arachne had chosen to weave was disrespectful to both gods and mortals alike. She had woven a picture that made fun of the gods. It made them look silly, ordinary, and very mortal!"

"And then?" Felix asked.

"You see, Arachne, by being so proud, had insulted all of the gods. Athena rose up in a fury and tore the tapestry from the loom. She struck Arachne on the head with the shuttle she had used for weaving. In that instant, Arachne began to feel her head grow smaller, her fingers and legs shrink until they were spindly. Like this." Edith raised one of her eight legs and waved it about for effect. "And Athena said to Arachne, 'Stupid, vain girl, go and spin your thread and weave not tapestries but empty nets, and learn

that the gods and goddesses must be worshipped properly by humans."

"The End?" Julep asked.

"Yes." Edith nodded and turned to look at Felix, who was very quiet.

Finally, he spoke. "May I make a comment on this story?"

"Certainly, Felix," Edith said. There was a slight tremor of anxiety in her voice.

"First of all, I am not a human. I am not a girl. And I already am a spider. So, from my point of view —" He paused. "From *our* point of view, this is not such a bad story. She was turned into one of us, a spider."

"True," Edith agreed.

"And second," Felix continued, "you have always told us that spiders have been around much longer than humans. We were here first — four hundred million years ago. So it isn't an accurate story."

"Myths are never accurate. We don't read them for accuracy. We read them to learn."

"I get it, Mom. I've learned." The words seemed to clog deep inside Felix. He could hardly go on, but he did. "And I won't brag, but please, just let me do my art. And . . . and . . . and . . ."

"And what, dear?"

"Remember, Mom, back when we were on our way to the Kontiki Antikies shop, I said I had something I wanted to bring up with you."

"Uh . . . vaguely, yes."

"You said, 'Later, when we're settled.'"

"So I did. Yes."

"Well, I know we're not exactly settled, but I would like to bring it up now."

"Certainly." Edith nodded.

The tiny hairs on Felix's front legs began to quiver.

"It's just that I feel I don't belong."

"Don't belong?" The entire web seemed to hum with Edith's alarm. "Whatever do you mean? We're a family. You belong right here."

"This is so hard to say, Mom. I feel that I belong with my family but not my species."

"What's he talking about?" Julep said.

"Ssshush!" Jo Bell said. At this moment, Jo Bell began to feel deeply sorry for her brother. Felix was different, but she loved him, and right now she felt as if he was about to turn their whole world upside down and inside out.

"Just because we're called recluses shouldn't mean we have to hide away!"

They were interrupted by a meow coming from the cabinet's back panel.

"Fatty?" Edith asked.

"Baggage backs up to the lavatories," Fatty said from a small air vent at the top of the cabinet. "Your creation is beautiful, Felix. Simply beautiful. And Felix is right. It truly is his name that condemns him."

"What's wrong with the name Felix?" Julep asked.

"No, dear child. It's the name of your species. Brown recluse," Fatty said softly. "Felix asks not to be judged by the poison in his fangs but by his character. As should each and every one of you."

Felix was overwhelmed. Fatty summed it up so well, so perfectly. All this time he had been wrestling with the dilemma. He could not deny who he was. "I want to live in the open," Felix declared.

"Felix, that is just too dangerous!" Edith was shaking so hard she could barely speak. "We can live in the open when we get to the Place Where Time Has Stopped."

"But that place might not exist. Mom, you're the one who always tells us to seize the day, to make the most of our lives. It is very hard to seize the day if we're always hiding. We never even see the daylight! And what good has hiding done us anyhow? I admit I was the reason we had to get out of the philharmonic, but no one had ever seen us at Kontiki Antikies."

"But they heard about us after the philharmonic hall incident!"

"It's no way to live, Mom!"

"Edith." Fatty began to speak. "You know how I care for you. But Felix is right. You could live in hiding, but should it be at the expense of your children?"

Edith was very quiet.

"Mom?" Felix finally said in a very tiny voice. "Mom, are you mad?"

"No, no, never. I'm just getting used to the idea."

"You mean — we can go out in the world?" Jo Bell asked. Every nano-hair on her eight legs trembled at the very thought.

Edith paused, looked at Felix, and then looked at each of her daughters. "Yes," she said. "It's just going to take me some time to get used to the truth that is before my half dozen eyes. Each one of my children has so . . . so much potential. And when we get to the Boston Public Library, you will find such inspiration!"

She turned to Felix. "Keep weaving, Felix,

keep spinning. It is beautiful what you are making — it's an astonishing creation." She paused. "Perhaps you could make us a lovely circle for circle time, you know."

"Oh, Mom, I'll make you the best web. My pleasure!"

SIXTEEN
The Boston Public Library

The next evening, Edith, her children, and Fat Cat disembarked at South Station in Boston.

"If I remember correctly, we can take the red line to Park Street and then the green line to Copley," Edith said.

"Wow, Mom!" Her children were impressed. Usually it was Fat Cat who handled public transportation.

"I know buses, your mother knows subways," Fatty said.

Within the hour they had arrived at Copley Square.

"Good gracious!" Edith sighed. "I get weak just looking at it!"

The Boston Public Library was a magnificent building. Despite its massive size, it seemed almost to float against the pink-streaked sky. The granite looked rosy and the arcaded windows had a golden luster. There was something timeless about it, Edith thought, and though it was not the Place Where Time Has Stopped, it held her family's future.

"It looks like a palace," Julep whispered.

"It is a palace!" Edith said as they climbed the granite steps to the front entrance. "But a palace for everyone. Look up, see the inscription."

"'Free to All'!" Felix read.

Two bronze statues guarded the entrance. "Who are they?" Julep asked.

"They are supposed to represent the arts and the sciences," Edith replied. "And look, there is a carved head right above the words 'Free to All.' Do you know who that might be?"

"Who?" Jo Bell asked.

"Athena."

"The goddess from the story — the one who turned Arachne into a spider!" Julep said.

"I hope she doesn't turn us into humans," Felix muttered as they skibbled through the front entrance and entered a huge vaulted space. A grand marble twin staircase faced them, with carved lions on pedestals at the first landing.

"There are forty-two steps to the first landing. I would suggest we float some lines to ascend."

Fat Cat slid between the cool shadows and crouched beneath another statue. The rich beige marble of the floor and walls offered a perfect camouflage for Fatty, whose fur was almost the same color.

The children could feel that the library was not simply a building but a world. Although Edith and her mother had lived in it for a long time, there were vast territories still unexplored. It had always been Edith's intention to visit the rare books room with her mother, Violet. But they never did. Violet was ill and grew weaker and weaker. With her strength ebbing, she simply could not make enough silk to scale the lofty peaks to the treasure trove that contained some of the oldest and most valuable books on earth. After Violet died, Edith had no stomach for going to the rare books room alone. But now, with three youngsters, it was the perfect expedition.

And so they began their ascent through the marble corridors, floating lines where they could to bronze statues or fixtures. They went up a final set of stairs and scuttled and skibbled down dimmer and dustier hallways until they stood in front of a set of double doors. In black letters were the words DEPARTMENT OF RARE BOOKS.

"I'm afraid this is where we part ways," Fatty said.

"Not for good," Edith replied. "I'll explore the ventilation system for you. There must be a way in."

"I'll roam around a bit. But you know, Edith —" There was something in Fatty's voice that made chills run through every one of the family's thirty-two legs.

Don't say it, Fatty. Please don't, Edith thought.

"You know," Fatty continued, "I'm more of a theater creature than a library one."

"No, Fatty! No!" the children cried.

"You've been with us forever," Felix said.

"You're like a dad," Julep whispered.

"You're family!" cried Jo Bell.

"She's right, Fatty," Edith said. "It makes no difference that you're a cat and we're spiders. You are family. In time of our trials, true, in the face of fear, faithful." They were all weeping now.

"And I shall always be." Fatty purred softly. "But the theater scene in Boston is good, and not far from here. I had a cousin who once played the Colonial Theatre — *The Lion King*, or it might have been *Wicked*. Not sure. I'll come visit. This isn't good-bye."

"You must let us know as soon as you have sett —" Edith caught herself before she said the word. "You must let us know which theater." She tipped her head toward the double doors of the rare books room. "But you know where you can find us."

"Yes, dear Edith."

"I understand from my late mother that they have some very early Shakespeare texts. Most likely I'll be there — sixteenth century."

"And you said that there are the letters and books of that magician fellow Who — whateee?" Felix asked.

"Houdini, Felix. Harry Houdini."

"That's where you'll find me, Fatty. The magic shelves."

"They have miniature books. Mom told me. Books no more than three inches high. A nice spider-size book, that's where I plan to be," Jo Bell said.

"Where will I go?" Julep asked. "Do they have a dollhouse like the one you told us about in the kindergarten room at the Martin Luther King Jr. Elementary School?"

Edith turned to her youngest. Her eyes gleamed. "They have something much better than a dollhouse."

"What?" Julep jumped up and down, so excited that she released a dragline.

"Pop-up books!"

"Pop-up books? What are those?"

"Books with movable parts. Some slide, some flip up or flap down — it's a whole tiny world in one book. There's a circus one. One has a ship on a sea with moving waves and sails. My mother — your grandma Violet — told me all about them. They have some of the oldest and best pop-up books in the world. And they still work!"

"Oh, wow!" the children all clamored.

"I want to go there!" Jo Bell said.

"Me, too!" Felix shouted.

"Mom, you said pop-ups are for me," Julep protested.

"There is plenty of room for all of you."

She turned to Fatty. "There's even one with a stage — the Globe Theatre. It's just paper. Make-believe," she said with a slight tremor in her voice.

Fatty crouched down so that he was very close to his dear friend.

"It's all make-believe, Edith."

EPILOGUE

And so Edith and her three children crept under the crack of the door and entered the rare books room of the Boston Public Library. They saw a man at a desk. Around his forehead was a band with a small light on it. He held a threaded needle in his hand and was bent over the pages of an ancient manuscript, which he appeared to be sewing together. There was a nutty odor of glue and wood swirling through the air, and just a tinge of mold. The man looked up from his work and peered in their direction.

"Freeze!" Edith commanded. The man peered harder. Edith was sure that he saw them, but he did not seem frightened. Not at all.

Then the most extraordinary thing happened. The man stood up and walked over to them. He bent down, and Edith's head swirled with confusion. Was he going to stomp on them? They couldn't scuttle away fast enough! She saw Felix float a line up to the rung of a desk chair.

"Welcome!" the man said. "I am so glad to see you. They tell me that book lice are quite tasty — tasty from a spider's point of view. There are plenty here. They eat paper. You will be doing a great service to the rare books collection if you would indulge yourself."

"Mom, what does he mean 'indulge'?" Julep whispered.

"Eat?" Jo Bell asked.

"You mean he's letting us stay?" Felix asked.

"He's not frightened at all. Isn't this lovely, children?"

"Is this the Place Where Time Has Stopped?" Julep asked.

"No, but I think we're getting closer," Edith said. "I think we can settle."

And so they did.

AUTHOR'S NOTE

As I'm sure you know, real spiders don't use words to talk. Nor do they read, nor do they wear hats as in Stephen Gilpin's wonderful illustrations. But here are a few things that are true about brown recluse spiders and the other animals that appear in this book.

* Spiders have multiple eyes — usually eight (except for brown recluses and their relatives, which have only six). In spite of all these eyes, most spiders do not see well.

* Spiders DO receive a lot of information through their ability to pick up vibrations. The tiny hairs on their legs work like motion detectors and alert them to the smallest movements.

✳ Spider blood is clear, with a bluish tint. This is because spider blood, unlike human blood, contains copper.

✳ Brown recluse spiderwebs look slightly blue.

✳ Spiders can regrow lost legs if they are still fairly young.

✳ Spider silk is much stronger than any rope or even steel cable that humans make.

✳ Pirate spiders, or Mimetidea, do eat other spiders.

✳ There really was a theater cat known as Boy Cat. He really did jump into the lap of the late Princess Margaret of England and eat the bouquet she was holding.

✳ There really was an infestation of hobo spiders, or *Tegenaria agrestis*, in the Pacific Northwest in the late 1980s.

✳ Finally, it's true that brown recluse spiders, like Edith and her three children, are very shy. But they can be very dangerous if they do bite. Their venom is toxic and causes necrotic wounds, which means that their bite causes human flesh to die. In some cases, brown recluse spider bites can be fatal. So enjoy reading about brown recluse spiders, but please — DON'T PLAY WITH THEM!